Howling Winds and Blue Tears

Forward H Makwavarara

Published by Mago Publishing, 2023.

HOWLING WINDS AND BLUE TEARS

First edition. December 17, 2023.

Copyright © 2023 Forward H Makwavarara.

ISBN: 978-1779333124

Written by Forward H Makwavarara.

Table of Contents

To Amai and Baba

To those who believed

A sleeping giant is not more useful than a corrupt midget. A ruined nation is their legacy.

Forward

The Crocodile Cries

Hard coated armoured back
Crafted to impervious defence
Canines menacing a snout to flinch
The cruel grip and death roll
Sluggish on dry land
Most menacing in deep waters
Who would love the crocodile?
I have heard of crocodile tears
The crocodile has no heart
What's in the water is fair game
Man hunts: his survival instincts
Do hunters have hearts I wonder?
Cut off and exiled under water
Who has lived in this habitat?
Who knows the pain of the crocodile?
Who knows it's loss?
Who cares when it cries?
When the crocodile cries
The waters wash it's tears away
Never to be seen by man's eye
Never has its pain been recorded
A truth is truth when there is testimony
Who testifies for the crocodile
Having no tongue to command words
Ostracised by man and beast
The lioness roars for her cubs
Who notices when the crocodile cries?
When a crocodile cries
It cries alone

The Land Cries

Her face awash with salt
It drained from eye fountains
And the fountains dried up
What drought ever was
When even the tears dry up
And that not only keen pain
Hearts torn up like old rags
Decomposing in murky despair
No needle and thread can mend
The tears of tattered heart fabric
Whose dream and hope is stolen
With tall stories and oratory
The tears ran dry on my face
The tears are deep and festering
Soon it will be only rot left
A country gone to barking dogs
Behind me baying bloodhounds
Pray winds blow in from behind
The hounds may lose my scent
Howling winds hasten escape
Blue tears of tattered heart
Cry the beloved country
This tear watered graveyard
Lament land of my heritage
Even my throat is parched
Proverbial betrayal - treachery
Tear me and shred me
Tears will not drown me
I am not dead yet

A Friend is Made

My friend, great man he is
A great hunter on good measure
In the day of his forays
Much meat he brings home
Calls me, neighbour, come eat
Make merry, drink the love of me
And I have a brother; wealthy Christian
Humble man I vouch for his heart
Bought he a suit and one for me
On Sabbath days am minded not to cook
His table flows drink and delicacy
He is better than drunken hunter?
No and No my children
You, have no friends such ostentation
To show you their bounty for your lack
A friend takes you to the hunt for spoil
A friend teaches the catching of fish
That his bounty is multiplied in yours
They which call you to after success party
Call your empty hands to more want
From such shy and find your means
And call a friend to go find his in your way
Then you shall have a friend
Who will supply your day of want
A friend, children, is the one made
That will feed you wisdom and off you
A friend will find you and teach you ropes
Bees have stingers but are kept
There's a way honey is made
Beekeepers eat of the sweet nectar

Good counsel is before the laughter
Such is before the wine is contemplated
Often followed of sweat and tears
Bad counsel brings rowdy pomposity
Often over the downing of the wine
Follow blood and tears; the death of it!

Asking for Time

Give me time you say
What is mine for giving
Not a mite would I withhold
How do I harness the brute
This rough shod smoothness
It's indifferent grind
Yet you ask me for time
Who is *Me* that should give time
Delay my justice deny my justice
Is it *just* that you ask such performance
Weigh me in your scales
Condemn me infirm beast
For such want is me
None my possession can't give
Aimless trudging and plod
Not knowing what you asked
You take time leaving me what?
Giving that you can't return
It's a waste and waste
Look my lost flesh
Only skin my hope
What is borrowed hope?
Clinging to shadows of sunset
Tomorrow might not come
Where would joy be born
For time given away today
Oblivion makes dark throne
Don't ask it of me
In usurpation would I grant
Was it frivolous presumption

That commits to such delivery
Did you hear yet?
I don't have time!

Drunk Behemoths

A moth came by the other day
As many moths have often done
And I had me a fire going
As it was night surrounding
And you know about moths
How they love landing on light
And this moth was drunk
So I called it beer-moth
And it's confidence compelling
So it thought of itself so big
And christened itself such
So named self; Behemoth
A beer-moth is no behemoth
A lesson learnt in flames of fire
Wings aflame a sure demise
Please moths don't come near
My fire is mine to tend
I would share but not with moths
I have me a fire so warm and hot
Her fuel the love I give full
Her reserve full and unquenchable
The twelve wells are in my heart
One every season the fire will burn
No its not for moths to love
I purposed it and fan a flame
What's her oil that she glows
Dispelling the dark shadows around
I carry the light season and out
And not moth nor mite I fear
Moths and beer-moths your peril

A Day in Years

The days make our lives
So we live them one a time
They add up a week to year
And we stand here with wonder
Then realisation smile
We have been gifted
And those around us chorus
Wishes of a brighter tomorrow
Basking in the glory of success
Jubilant poets in recitals
And the gifted musicians serenade
Dream dreams little one
Is it the happiness of love you seek
Or perhaps the comfort of goods
To go out in peaceful war mornings
To return riding a gelding of success
Dream on and dream it little one
Then rise a conqueror your dream
What would I wish you today
Except your dream and more
Make merry and make myrrh
Let me embrace you as treasure
Greatest value and esteem of many
Receive the denouement of wisdom
Good things, Wonderful things
Good dreams, Wonderful dreams
Sweet peace, Wonderful peace
Dream, love, laugh
Ah happiness
Happy another birthday friend!

Bony Hope

Not residents of the necropolis
Bones rise sweat flourish
Spring of fountain of sweat
Look into the future-scope
What says the sign...tell it
My bones, my bones I swear
And make oath in honey pots
It is not a vow made in wine
Make choreography virtuoso
These bones shall bear fruit
Yes, the arrogance of my hope

Drunk Melancholy

Of stingers, singers and sinners
The stinkers and sinkers are many
Tinkers and thinkers not far off
Benders and menders create legends
Maggots, bigots and idiots ensemble
To tell storeys tall stories
Fixers and mixers a drunken world
Making matting sense in scents and cents
Blindness bundles bounties of naivety
Screened screams of the creamed
As the joy will buoy the profits
Downright simpletons; naive you and me
For entertainment albeit internment
I could I would blame them
Milk of lofty folly profit of the ilk
Was no way better to commit our profit
We stink and sink to our want
They think, we stink
They sing and sting to the bank
Tinkers, Benders menders are busy
Painting shame and vice so nice
The gullible babble and drink some more
Melancholic alcoholic
I drink too!

For Kate Chopin

I guess I am crazy but I'm not
But I should have married Kate
Convention through the window
It is great slavery of the will
But Kate Chopin rude realist
And indeed life goes on without you
Ah! I should have married Ms Chopin
She would not dote over me
Neither in life nor in dole of death
Embracing her new found freedom
In stride carry on with life
Such an encumbrance social rectitude is
Kate Chopin should I have married
Scarce would she mourn death
Life is for the living - the free
Whose will bends to no man
Nor woman at that
Such unabashed pragmatism
But would she have married me?
Even I wouldn't want tears my wake?
Perhaps only for giving her will
To blow like the wind lists to do
Giving her blue skies in cloudy season
Were marriage open prison home
Knowing her, if she expired would I mourn?
And expiate our expedient hypocrisy
And find bitterness in honey what sweet pepper
And such incongruity is human emotion
Oppression of love's noble intentions
What romanticism we would revolt against!

Four words God, only six

In the days that God remembered us
And in his multitude of grace and love
Did He to us that we might testify
And sing our joys unlimited His goodness
For a double portion of His blessing
So a man child to us was given
And a girl child completed our joys
The sun rises and we count our blessings
And for twins we count it double
Our mouths are filled with laughter's song
The lily of the valley is scented no sweeter
Than the thought that God blessing blest us
See them to grow in wisdom and love
And may your ways be their paths
Where on light leads the way of joy
Peace only from the springs above
A perfect river to quench thirst
And wash the little feet of joy bundles
Again asking they see many days
With abundance of corn and wine their fields
What is a perfect prayer from a parent?
Year after seasons another day comes
Like a statute of remembrances
Counting and reminiscing anew
In you the Great God we place hope
In a few words let the fullness suffice
The greatest prayer I shall mouth
God, bless my children
Male and female your creation
Another day another year this my song

At day break and even tide shall pray so
In the lightness of joy raising same word
Weary and sombre at evening I to sigh
Let just these four words escape my lips
God bless my children
And today allow me six words
God bless my children, all equal

Good Neighbours

Once ago I found me good land
A good portion of goodly land it was
Fenced it off proofed wildlings
Peace at last and sleep came easy
Then upon a time by fortune
A neighbour did come up
Fenced off his portion against mine
Bounds set strong we acquainted
In good speech neighbourly ways
In hushed industry did termite colony thrive
Mildew and rust partnership unholy
Cracks appeared then breeches
A sheep keeper I have been
My neighbour a breeder of dogs
He, a good man, till then
I shot a dog for spooking the flock
Words we spoke over the fence
Harsh words don't mend fences
My neighbour sensible man
Made a fence his side
A good new fence, a strong fence
The other day I gave him lamb
A good fence is goodly neighbours boon!

Heart Aches

In the valley of deep shadows
Feeding drenched to the bone
There was a storm last night
The rain just let up now
Looking to the eastern skies
The sun is rising again
Hope of seeing flowers in bloom
And bees busy with nectar intent
We will have honey this year
So I will bide my time
It's all I hold
And then came the quake
What Richter's scale could measure?
Rocking my being a ragdoll
I was looking wrong
In the rain did not see day pass
I am looking west
It is a setting of the sun!
Darkness deeper than shadows
Time given in all hope
Now to solitude and oblivion
Sweet stinking sadness!
Whiskey sting me -
Please!

Hindsight

Gifted like many in hindsight
I never saw it coming till catch-up
Naivety and gullibility of the heart
This little choice and that other
Riding desire's chariot of the blind
Choice on present taste depends
In captivity now pain deepens
To say all this; life in dippings
So in little choices a compass set
The road taken is predestination?
Boy do we score own goals our rout
The danger is in the heart not eye
'The acids of euphoria ever brew
Chase, chase, chase, chase, chase it
The hunter glories in the catch
Excellence is not in chasing
It is a sword of two edges
You chase what you will
You eat that you kill
Wrestling is heroic sport
To wrestle an asp is folly
The venom is not in size
Beware hypodermic fangs
These dipping is my story
And so honey is very sweet
But the bee carries a stinger
Chase the Holy grail
Is it even holy or real?
Slumber is not an option
But don't run unshod over thorns

Prepare the hunt prepare the race
I went hunting: the vixen looked easy
I have scars
It depends
Read my story
It deepens
Write your story
Suddenly I live
Another race, a new race
Informed hunt.
For;
Desire is the chariot of the blind
Vision drives the successful

Untamed Thievery

Of writing verse what's conscience
In words sometimes pouring inspired; heart
Often times insipid concoctions
The knock boards stand in ovation
Politeness often trumps truth
Perhaps to change the sound boards
Are verse writers all so convicted
Serving their ditch water shamelessly
Is there a word that rings without heart?
Lies, truth and yes, bland formalisms
Who captures the dreary efforts
When commerce is the exigence
And wit labour's daily pitchfork
They say to make hay in sunshine
Met for the belly politics
Who will tell the truth of words
The author feels to broach public
The hearer chooses the connotation
A chancy reconciliation of mind worlds
Persuasion is an art - a thievery of sorts
Thus I steal your eyes to share mine
Do I see dimly - not your eyes
The brilliance of oratory aptitude
Poets, politicians, publishers, their ilk
Are they not opinion benders?
Well and ill intended what's the difference
Entrapment is denial of freedom
A subversion of judgment; yours
Then you pay the price of discipleship
Often compromising independent thought

Where did I start? for I digress
Were these words inspired
Perhaps by greed and mongery
Are they inspiring as wished in me?
Perhaps most insipid and bland
So you see, your chaste thought
Engaged to work at stone-bang
What is gained save to serve me
And crown me lord of thought
Even that were just for a moment
Yet you can't stand in derision
Proverbial hypocrites as *Literary Critics* maybe
You too seek your profit; bread (even ill)
In purported insight my protestations
Let me rest to brew again in time

Inspiration

The mother watches with glee
She has waited, watching
Sitting, teething, crawling
Stand ungainly; step, step
The beginnings of valour
Baby steps nomenclature
The simplicity of truth
Baby steps made Pheidippides
Baby steps don't look back
Never crawl again, step and run
No giant, not a warrior or runner
But all took the road ungainly firsts
Dadle, fall and laugh hard
Dadle, fall harder cry loud
Steady feet are not borrowed
Yours will carry you your desire

Lioness Birth

One day who had known
Yet many expected and we are fulfilled
Had we dreamed had we wished
Who would have known the gem
So precious that superlatives
And all adjectives would fall short
How do you bind value and beauty
Then use words to describe such
I stand here in beaten silence
To the awesome Lioness that's here
In her roar fills the air so sweet
In her presence the Lords lose reason
At a distance hearts quake in longing
The stars of heaven join in testimony
And shadows bend in obeisance
What honour befits this apparition
That I hold so dear to heart today
And sing a song that no words pronounce
It is a song of eternal hope
Profound and primordial to reason
May your days know only one face
The face that smiles lighting your ways
That you may walk only to success
Arms that bring on joy and good things
Embrace and enfold you in good health
Your transport be only wings of joy
Taking you to fountains of flowing peace
Wisdom be a fountain in your heart
That all your craft may profit
What would I ask for you had I one wish?

That your days in goodness may be long
Today we smile in song
Celebrating your days thus far
Wishing you so many more
We embrace you in love
And dream with you for you
Your tomorrow be greater than now
Happy blessed birthday princess

Lizards and Rodents

Your place in the Ark taken by a pig
Noah did not discriminate against any
Peter struggled with discrimination
Green leaf... new life on earth
One year in the Ark
What fear assailed Noah and family?
When will this rain stop?
When will the flood subside?
Ask "I will heal their land"
Sodom and Gomorah must be destroyed
So that God may make things new
Noah and Family
Lot and Family
Christ and the church
Rebellion in the house
Ham, Lot's wife and Children
Did you not hear the story
Lizards and rodents entered an ark
And a man – real human
Did not crush their heads
Gave them grain their meat
Saw them off rewilding
You discriminate a soul
Your shame!
Clean up clean up clean up
Put away the confusion wine
Who has not been drinking here
Kings, Priests and their Princes
And their wanton women no better
We may yet hope again?

Mirror the Faithful

Mirror, mirror oh how so faithful you are
Queens and princess have trusted you
They have painted faces and plaited hair
Fashionistas have planted hairs and shaved
How many are encouraged for surgical plastic
Because you, o mirror are so faithful
You tell the story as it plays out
History was never your fancy, you are present
Testify and testify again faithful witness
They will doctor evidence high and low
You reveal the sins of the present man
Indeed, mirror you, a law unto yourself
Who shall ever adjudge you a liar
Unmoved and unshaken a wrinkle reveal
Creases on un-ironed aging skin suit
Paste it over and brush will blush matt
Faithfully revealing our real estate
Some landscaping that you tell
Many hate their truth bared
So many settle for truth barred
Would you blush your penchant for truth
Dear Mirror

River Ministry

There were two men and mighty
The one whirlwind and ferocious
The other a river mighty and ravenous
And they still live today
One is you and other is me
Now who is you and who is me?
See I give you the option
The whirlwind came in violence
Danced the war dance in fury circles
Picked all the rubble it's mighty could
Tossed everything skyward
It went there and thither there again
Would someone direct it's pursuit
Make construct of this violent endeavour
A trail of destruction in its wake
Even trees uprooted in their fruit
And houses stood roofs ripped off
Passage blocked across many roads
The joy of many a distorted shambles
Hurt is come in the wind - a man!
Carrying and blowing to waste!
Was that not you crushing me dead?
The river it's course determined
Ran with patient determination
Impediment encountered new course cut
Circumvent and charter to destine
In bouncing wave wash a path
A pebble carried to deposition sooner
Only in its course defying harness
Silently snaking beauty bound seaward

Watered plains and green banks
A testimony of benevolent history
Visitation was for all thirsty life
Sublime moments a bird sings appreciation
A fruit feast overhangs the bank
Cool weary feet and bless parched throats
Relief both gentle prey and mean hunter
Neutral grace that has no favourites
The true minister that I would be

Seeing you

I see you because
You want me to see you
Yet I don't see you
Because you want me to
Wish I wouldn't
When you would not
See you through
See through you
Sight!
Sigh!

Tears and Tears

What are these tears you shed
The cicada for its incessant cry
Mourns the heat of day
Does it sleep when night falls
Does it hope for a new day
Perhaps its daily prayer for rain
Then a season comes to pass
The cicada's faith vindicated
A nation of cicadas?
What are these tears in this raiment
Much flesh is bared – fashion?
More wear and tear evinced
The elements have not spared
How shall they dress this poverty
Their song laments unemployment
What hope for the fruit of own sweat
A continent of beggars

Tearing Hearts

Have you torn our hearts from their bosom
As a rapist humbling our hopes and dreams
And rape as oft committed by non-strangers
To walk away in defiant impunity
Just because you are the chosen?
Of a truth, there was no forced entry
Just the worst betrayal of trust
As when an uncle on brother's daughter
It is easier to win enemies to love
Than a brother lost in betrayal

The Seer

This was a dream,
Most strange dream
And there it was I stood on a hill outcrop
Cast my eye in the distance
No enemy was found near or far
A sunshine most beautiful
Filtered sweetly through branch and leaf
Bathing me in pure ecstasy
Golden shimmer almost palatable
That it were possible to keep memory
And this strangeness in all grace
Did give way to an eastern sunset
The shimmering glow burning copper
The silhouettes of the hills bowing
There reverence most eloquent speech
Da Vinci and cohorts could not blend
The visual music of my witness
The hills in worship dreamily swayed
An almost imperceptible morning greeting
And there mesmerised almost a worshiper
Who would not be converted?
I am a village boy and uncultivated
I have bathed in seasons drizzles fine
Once have I seen ground hoar
Yet now on my perch a horror
Apparition of clouded sky approaches
Burnished copper in tinges of gold overtaken
A mass menacing whitish grey
A cloud of frost belching silent rage
Preceding an obtuse wall of hoar stone

Too brittle for snow too deliberate for ice
Yet the menacing advance!
It must come near still so high tail
There must be shelter westward
Sounding alarm of coming outrage
Inclement weather accompaniment
Sound a warning in the city by fireside
Their barely sustained comfort won't cut
Flee for the cause of your life
A child I think was motherless
My pressing a man: hoary head and beard
A rescue of grace most touching
An Ark of horses stands by the city gates
A basket on wheels to a place yonder
A voice of hope spoke of distant place
Inclement weather trudged defiant
A team of horses, white horses most unperturbed
Of sure step over compacted white sheets
Brutal ice would offer firm step
There is a lighthouse out there
An encampment that is sure comfort
The elements shut out of its confines
Wait out the indecent onslaught
Till the copper shall burn a sunrise
And give way again to the gold and silver
So shall we live and love again.
The politics of hope - hope of politics?

There is a Way

There is a way if you would look
When they stand in your way
Mountains flint and granite
Un-giving and uncooperative
Your quest on the other side
Three things you can do, ay four
And the fourth unconscionable
Brute force; chisel hammer and spade
It is only rock; can't defy you
On the other side shall light be
Learn from the mole who needing no light
Carrying neither hammer, chisel nor spade
Tunnels hard earth for habitation
Gnawing, clawing and pushing dirt
Brute force, no chivalry
Such grit never say die
Dreams are a flighty bird
Give yourself wings and fly over the barrier
The great eagle is propelled in air
Passion is a wing: a flap at a time
Rising above peaks for prey yonder side
And a battle eagle's war cry, a happy hunt
And yet are not all eagles and brutes
The fox is most cunning hero and villain
Subject of much folklore
Eavesdropping by its den lesson learnt
Work smart said it to its brood
Why take a mammoth head on
Circle its blind side it is not your prey
He that is neither brute, mole nor fox

The terror of the ostrich head in the sand
Would wish away the obstacle day
Till we succumb in white boned skeletons
An obituary of dreams that never tried
If only I had a leg, a wing or chisel
Think it; the fox has neither strength nor flight
Yet to its foothills den brings prey of yonder side

Thinking Thanking Mother

A mother is so for birthing
A mother is so for nurturing
A mother is so for providing
You have Mothered again today
You were a mother yesterday
We are grateful in your gracious ways
Suckled in your love
Comfortable on your shoulder
Mother yesterday, today and tomorrow
May we like you be mothers one day
Thank you Mother
Our hearts are full
We are truly grateful!
My tears run wash eyes
They bath the heart love renewal
These little waters of felicitous fountain
Mother was crying for joy
Cried in birth pains I was told
And cried again at first cuddle
Then the growing came
She cried nights for sickling me
Did you know my first poem?
Boy did mummy cry happy
Then I left home it was for school
And my embrace mummy cried
Coming home song stood there
And did you know, mummy cried
Now I know that is motherly business
And mothers have the fount
A spring so clear and sometimes serene

Where only tears of joy bubble
And am here mama, a kiss
You remember baby kisses mama?
They still live here in my heart
Untainted by age defying geography
Here mama, a kiss for you
I know you will cry again
The business of love
But don't cry mama
See, we cry too, just like you!
I guess we have learned the ropes
That bind in infinite love
The tears; the drops of love!

Village Boy's Lily

The princess of all flowers
The fragrance of the valley
The Unparalleled beauty
Adorning the veld in charm
Of delicate petals promise
A call to the nectar within
The honey bee sings all day
Perhaps drunk of the sweetness
Yes. I saw the lily of the valley
And my heart left the mountains
Now it resides in the valley
Waiting to see the budding and blooming
The smiling purity of nature
Keep the valley watered and fed
Let the Lily grow unfettered
Hearts will know peace
In the valley of the water lily
And a village boy wandering the hills
Duty herding a small herd village cattle
And my village tastes for natural beauty
Witnessing the cocky defiance
Face to face with delicate loudness
The flame lily's commanding presence
Nor would hesitate to pluck the bloom
Some vivid rage red so passionate
The cousin not so blatant yet noticeable
Maroons often tinged with yellow arrogance
Who blames a lily for making a statement
Were it not endowed would acclaim come
That a nation would make an emblem

I bet you have not seen the bloody lily
Its scandalous spiky bloom enchanting
Such lovable vulgarity yet so delicate
The Zimbabwean summer's presents
Only a village boy gets to witness
But yet no loss to metropolitan
National Geographic Channel your hope
You can boast of the scientific nomenclature
So you pay to watch these mirages
But the village boy's ignorance has touched
And takes for granted, another season comes

Wine Tester

Watching the stars of southern skies
Invasion of innocent conscience
A flood of strange light mind seat
Breaking the spell milky way cast
What mischief is this cloud
Sublime opioid season so transient
a smile fluttering; my youth renewal
Might the days of love and dance
Perhaps be my guest again?
Awake and away blasphemous thought
Age a jubilee and embrace the real
This cloud has no rain
Don't rip earth and plant seed
Forget new corn and new wine
They say it tastes better matured
Store it in barrels of fine oak
Drink a centenary tastes better
I have been a wine tester...
Tasting an aging year at a time!

Yellow is Red?

We are yellow outside
That is what you see
We are darker inside
See my dark skin
Brown earthy colour
A child of the soil
My pride is inside
Yellow makes you see red
I laugh loud I laugh long
Cracked, coughing, spitting
It is not for merriment
I am tired of mourning
You stole joy now I rage
Hills awake red earth
A teapot shaped nation
Spouting hot blood
And yellow went livid
The crocodile is on dry ground
Jaws and tail a little help
The hunter rules the land
Strike the soft belly
Crocodiles are yellow bellied
Drain the putrid pools
Expose, expose say expose
You build your walls high
Fenced your Vilenesses inside
That we may not see you naked
In time we have grown tall
Even on our knees we see inside
Though we were blind as bats

To think you were our brothers
Till treacherous trickery found you
And now we are yellow
You see us; red!

*The greatest prayer for success is called
planning, and the greatest answered
prayer for success is called work.*

Forward

The Woman

The gold of the morning
Catches her back
Bent in toil
The silver gleam
Punishes and slowly roasts
Her water salt turns
She stretches her back
Wipes her brow
A back hand mix
Granules of dust and her salt
Looks at hers
With gentle toil pressed eyes
Smiles her assurance
It shall be well
Even tide catches a weary step
Trudging towards the sunset
To make a fire
Boiled vegetables and "sadza"
Mother's love the cooking oil...

...Never sleep tummy empty

Gathered around the fire
Stories told and shared laughs
United, happy-what's more?
The songs would come
Supplications made to on high
She taught us to pray
Not a night passed
A prayer for her hatch.
True balm for weary bodies
Tomorrow will be soon
God bless my children
It is well with my soul
Then came tomorrow
With more gold her herald
Our heads bowed to receive
The golden fingers
Touching and warming
Our toil stained bones
For we worshiped backs bent
At the altar of the brute
Call it hard work
Now tomorrow is here
Her gold here blooms
We collect of her silver
The brute a beauty
A psalm and joyous song
For the supplication of the woman
And she has not stopped
Age's lines etched in her beauty
A smile telling of patient faith

The greying head and slowing step
Yet more sure and resolute
Continues to rally her progeny
A bastion and bulwark our fortitude...

...Farm light

Till in bad light
Risk your wheat
A farmer rises with dawn
To welcome the light
At one with the crop
Man meets nature
To perpetuate it
That he may
Of nature be nurtured
True light brings understanding
For lack of knowledge we perish
Search nature to teach you
It holds all secrets of human voids
Not by freaky chance
But principled order.

Mirth in death

I cried when you went away
Loneliness my comfort?
I did not mourn
You would come back
In death we will go
I will mourn to celebrate you
That you were my joy
Yet I will follow suit
For yet a little while
To equal you estate
No dirge in marriage
Yet shall be mirth In death?
Possibly?

WWW.World

What cares do you have?
And who cares you do?
A wild world what home?
They ride, they fly
They sailed, now they surf
O what village a wide world
Man with no use of woman
Woman to other preference
The world not weird?
I have seen it all wide world
They do it all wild the world
Many things I don't grasp so weird?
Wild, wide, weird, World
Whatever, wherever, whoever, Whenever
Yeah don't give up.

No Balls

We were young then
Played in the streets
Had our balls............
Grew up left the streets
Lost our balls.
Fear the streets
Where is comfort zone?
Survival wasted in youth
The old won't go to play
Ah I know!
They don't have balls!

Tears in The Wind

I have sown my tears in the wind for you
In the wind they have been buried
I, emptied, dried, parched
Looking to the skies
In a daze
Faint
Hope they collect and condense somewhere
To fall as dew drops in some valley
Wetting the ground we walk
Sprouting the full hope
Dreams prayed
Sweet
I have loved a life and lived little of it
Much loved yet so little to show
Dreams fade vivid memories
Yesterday is come today
Live for me now
Heart
This sad song for the graveyard of hearts
Mine buried for love and country
Carry me eagle in the wind
Let us find my tears
Water this future
Faith

Your offense

In truth I swear
To your offense do I
Yet not to spite
Your Respectable-ship
High regard your esteem
Moth I and behemoth you
What harm could pass
From my moth-ship
Yet a moth-hood
Shall see your demise
For you offend truth
I swear you offend!

Apparition

A day and a dream
That I would if could have kept
A moment so fleeting
With sublime delicacy
Yet what permanent imprint
Clutching at vapours
Sinking in desperate sea
That baptism of desires
That faith no fulfilment
And feigns not commitment
Kisses of an Angel
Or brushes of perdition
That tug and twist hearts
Brings us to submission
Dreams hope and fear.

Parched – Global warning

Wetlands sucked long of a desperate monster
All similitude humanoid
Engineered tentacles how cunning
You sapped me your supper
Licked your lips and burp
Kill the duck get the egg
Shouted in childish glee
Soon forgot tomorrow
You counted yesterday now
Yet you will come again
With new hunger to sup
See my cracked face
Stench of death perfume
My cracked giggle a dry laugh
Natural to nature to laugh last
No water up and down
Am parched................ .
You capitalist unbridled!

Vagabond King Dog

Dogs and men went a party
Kings and vagabonds came
Such pomp and ceremony
Choice meats for the kingship
And entourage of kissers
Wine mixed happy hearts condescending
Kick the last vagabond to darkness
Choice crumbs and morsels
What kindness feed my dogs
Kick out the dogs, kick good
Dogs and vagabonds kindred
In darkness burry them
The honour of a dog
The dishonour of a vagabond
Feed the worms the carrion
A dog in a casket, guns, salute
Vagabond's unmarked anthill earth
Inconvenience of kissers and kings
Then once upon a day come
A meal served on a hearse of guns
Ah at last a kingly meal
Kissers in attendance and Kings
In plates golden and silver casket
Sighed the hungry worm,
"Tastes like vagabond dog"
O my, such insolent eater!
Bring them on vagabond, king, dog
Ceremony does no impression
Such rude uncouth indifference
Serve the table of gluttony

Who was preferred none
To the worms to the worms
Same table instrument equity
To munch a snack vagabond
Was it a king or his dog?
Ironic insolence!

Cheat cheat

What is the score?
Would you settle for less
For honesty, If there was more?
Which devil would you serve?
You navigate mine fields
With art and deceit
To your wound and gripe
I've been there too
Walked a tight rope no audience
It was slippery
Now broken bones my shame
Ah an audience at last
They spit tears and fury
The sweet is bitter root
They will heal perchance
So away to court oblivion
Salt waters wash my eyes
Keep me from shadows and cupboards
Haunted by skeletons
Wishing I won't be found
Close my eyes tight
Bite my lips to bleed
Rattle not rattle not the past

Born First

First among equals, who holds your hand
Ominous sceptre thrust in your hand
And staggered drunken from its weight
With little steps and unsure gait
Two legs good we are equals stagger
Three legs better you are first steady
Hind foot shall follow the fore
And in his train shall many suit
Rope them and keep them in the fog
Gather them in dark cold nights non stray
And your embers fails not of warmth
Man child has been thrust fatherhood
You reign the king's heritage vice and virtue
Standing in scarred feet planted even
Knowing compassion and deliver justice
Then to be counted progenitor's pride
And your name seeker and gatherer
You are a planter's son and marvel
The equals shall be puffed in you humility
The glory seen in branches that bloom
The humility of the stem rooted
Searching the deep unfathomed dark
Nourish and water the branch to seed
Steady and fast the sceptre of first
First among equals and still equal
This succession of kingdoms prospered
How be it some floundered heritage lost
And names went windward
For the first more equal than kin
And staggered drunk to the drowning

Stand the gales and stem the floods
Unmoved
Unshaken
Steadfast
First among equals 'tis purposed!

Phon(e)ication

We *community-cated* once ago
It was joyous events
Desire to touch trudged miles
Family rituals each day conversed
Gossip and mischiefs whispered taboo
Daughters and women learned motherhood
And fatherhood the dream of boy manhood
Devised mouth to ear resuscitation
And indeed so personal pride
Of generation past to posterity
Then the earth was vast boundlessness
Quest to uncover and happenstance conquer
Time honoured sled to revered Apollo
And that was the story of our device
The personal community turned global
And personal hearts turned common good

Weary feet and honourable effort
Memory of visit paled in perfunctory holla
The snobbery ostentation of *phonication*
With liberal pervasiveness to perversity
Right there under your nose
Scent and stench in mischievous mix
The pungent odourlessness of vice
Let me bewail a lost son
My brother a wife and sister husband
We all kneel on her altar goddess phonication
Her sting a wasp hid in honeycomb
Lick the honey till taste a sweeter venom

And we reach for the horizon
Exert hard on the bounds of decency
In wanton creativity new diction coin
"Sexting" was my creamer a "sex-sting"
Can I begin to tell of abbreviation!
The worship continues new converts rise
Hook them up and rob them time
Conveniently connected thoroughly disconnected
My son had 666 friends all bodiless
Now claims 999 a day later
They are all on face register some fake
A knitted brow, I watched his face
A smile, a chuckle and more texting
At 17 I had lost him in my presence
He worshiped the uncanny goddess
My daughter was next to go 16
Victims of connected disconnection
Now I mourn another 14, a son
Good things hoped on generation to generation
Delivered from generation to degeneration
Evolution passed over revolution revolting
In stink heaps of death and destruction
Swift publicity from ghost to coast
So was vicious atrocity as never celebrated
Birthing the Arab Spring that was no spring
Scandal and disaster great merchandise
My neighbour's daughter was a saint
Till vice found her antics porn stardom
Victim of lust filled man a social shame
My acknowledgement I have seen good
My confession is quantum vice amidst virtue
More hearts break salty water of eyes

It's the new normal of phonication
My neighbour, a brother newlywed
Signature I DOs still in wet glimmer
Ink of certification barely dried
To sexting another was wife given his dismay
The eloquent hurt hate fashioned
It was on the rocks barely consummated
An exposure of shame unexpected
Alas *phonication* of shame
These be your phones
Whose smartness brought you out of ignorant bliss
The ones that were far off to new closeness
Tearing the close to push furthest
Curled up and cosy moral hibernation
A summer of decadence thawing what's left
Our moral core in atomic decay
Alas we are all *phonicated*
The ignorance of a rat relishing nuts in trap
Whoever condemned nuts? they are food
This my greedy lust and appetite a trap
By my fathers, I swear on it sir
I am shut, trapped in *phonication*

Burn again

It was the day from space
That brought floods from oblivion
Honey rivers flowed again
So honey buckets were filled
The sweetness of yesterday
I lick my fingers and dentures melt
Bridle time and guide it back
Carry me back wonder moments
To a resurrection of fire
Burn again my bosom
The fuel of unrequited passion
I will yet live again re-live
Don't delay awake and come
This waiting!

Word Spill's pen

Wakey wakey sleepy heads.
No time for slumber
Stretch and yawn a day
Embrace pen canon
A fountain spray your heart
Are you yet dry as Sahara
That you are silenced as church
I pray a renewal in word
Your feelings of days gone
Was it your hope in neuter tomorrow
Are you passed out in the grind
Off your laurels shake dust
As power assegai spills blood
Pick pen and spill the ink

Am singing a solo
Were it not a quartet of voices
I was happy in the medley of fools
They knew to cry and laugh
Please

Drink a river

And the rivers flowed
And the Honey never stopped
In the darkest nights
The crystals glowed golden
In winter refused freeze
The sea filled the rivers
And the streams perennial
Love's unquenchable flow
Drink your daily thirst
The waters are here
Let honey rivers flow
Perchance we fill our buckets
Insatiate as yet we are
Drink and drink

I filled the cup again

To God, glorious Omniscient and Omnipotent
My glory stands in the substance of your grace
For my quiver is filled with your goodness
And the pride of a parent with goodly children
Today shall I not pray again as I did yesterday?
I lift up my voice to your mountain in awe
To sing a song of thanks giving and delight
For you have again granted them another day and year
Was it of merit your glory would human share
But for your favour are we truly thankful
Walk daily Lord in their valleys hold them in comfort
And in their weakness shore them uphill
On their mountains be the humbling breeze
In their victories gratefully acknowledge your power
And days that you ordain to come their way
Shall turn times into years to greyness of head
A fullness of your flagon of abundance
Refill it daily with wisdom and discernment
Health be only good and prospering their hands
Are their houses empty?
Fill them with laughter
Are their arms shortened?
Yours are beyond measure
Are their voices faint?
Your ears are not stopped
When they are lost, You see in solid darkness
Have I asked for too much Lord?
My trust is in your bountiful supplies
Have I asked for too much Lord?
My confidence you know the very best

In my ignorance and waywardness
I am just a parent grateful to you for them
And am just a child supplicating a father
Humiliate me Lord and raise a standard
That your presence be seen ruler supreme
Commanding their ways to a glorious day
These that you gave to me are yours
Thy Divinity, guide thou their journey
To a divine consummation in your will
To dwell in the shadow of your presence

Clara's prayer:

Restore

A time of liberty
Proclamation of rest
Freedom from bonds
Signing for properties
Restitution
Restoration
Jubilee
Crowning of life offers
May it all be yours
And more
Happy 50 years
My baby brother

Humble Town

Fifty and no turning back
That's a jubilee of years
What jubilation must overtake
What freedom must come
Of a truth a little apprehension
Does time fly so quickly
Over my shoulder see first grade
Or was it yesterday college
A father that became
Three times grandfather now four
How fugitive time flies
One foot I have made start
Gunning a second Pentecost
The spirit is defended
Tongues of fair light the way
I will yet hope anew

With love besieging all round
What wish else would come
Comfort, comfort me
I haven't given it
Yet received of you and you
I know family gives more
So you did and took less
Humble Town my new residence
Where else would I be
But here surrounded
The joy of this family!

Still here

I loved a woman unforgettable
It was summer in a cold country
The season changed it was winter
The country was still cold
But my fire was hotter
But what is a fire without bread
The season freezing the gardens
In starvation distance did damage
Yet I love today as last summer
Summer comes and winter goes
And as yesterday my dreams
I will hold on in long lone patience
And sing a song Do You Believe Me Now!!!

Go conquer

And my perception says there is a sky
Then the gunner, a war man took task
Went skyward and broke the clouds
Was there a sky found to stand?
There are worlds unknown in the beyond
Galaxies and constellations abound am told
And they not constrained in within
Was it that possibilities are limitless
And perhaps it's my finite comprehension
And I will yet break the limited sky
To soar high above clouded margins
Not anymore shall the sky limit
And the airman shall testify

The sky just a vertical horizon
I say; set new horizons
Son don't go get the horizon
Son go push the horizon
And take an aerial view
You are born a conqueror

Hurting child

Mouth keep my peace
The children have spoken
A song of weddings and funerals
Some loves die unmade
One loved and not laughed
What?
Whose promise questioned
Dreams of shared hopes
To fruit in child gift
Was this all a lie?
Testimony of happenstance
Of love once lived
Now embers and shadows
Categorical fools child endangered
Love's miscarriage tears
They hate, they hurt they ....

De-Tongued: Hold not your peace

I went to a tailor today after so long
And it was not to patch my pants
I ordered a steel zipper rust proofed
The tailor had non to spare
Couldn't bridle my tongue
The butcher is my daily offense
Today for gory meats his victuals
Cut out my tongue with glee
I would have zipped quiet
But now I mourn my tongue
Voiceless you shall yet hear
Crying yet louder above your canons
Bring your craft oppression and suppression
My mouth shall bleed incessant
You didn't know?
The din of canons and sirens
That is children's dance class
My silence will scream hornets
My blood drown a tsunami
My pain will roll an avalanche
Till the salamander tail regrows
And my tongue is back in place
You will see red waste I bleed
I dare your menacing countenance
Though you may kill me for it
Would I not have sung for you!
Would I not have ululated!
But you multiplied pain
You killed the beauty of dreams
Stole their future

My generations after me cry
Cut my tongue again
I am the root of your discomfort
But my branching shall have tongues
They will wail their anguish
And scream incensed rage
They will see your most sorry end!

Dedication

I know a girl but I don't know her
She is a great girl but I don't know her
She inspires greatly but I don't know her
Forget your feast Days coz I don't know her
Name a day after her and the world will know her
Were it my power, would name a day to Her
Yes, I would call it Her day
Then today I would say "Happy Girl Day"
That will be the day I know her
To etch her memory to eternity
But today I don't know her still
Yet to put a smile on her face
And perhaps be filled in her radiance
I will break taboo and praise her virtues
Sadly, I don't even know her Name......

Life; as if I knew

What is life?
I wonder
Who has seen its face?
To see God?
I've searched for it, I can't find it
Yet I live it daily
Does it have a heart?
They say it is cruel
I *wonder* perhaps wander!
Does it have a direction?
They say look to the future
For some it is directionless
Yet for some, to great heights it soars
For some, to dark oblivion it grinds
To some it surfs to greatness
Yet for others it grinds
And grinds
For no one will it wait
It surfs
Cool breeze
And serves
Hard hand
... life

You ask for time

Give me time you say
What is mine for giving
Not a jot would I withhold
How do I harness the brute
With its rough shod smoothness
It's indifferent grind
Yet you ask me for time
Who is me that should give time
Delay my justice deny my justice
Is it *justicable* you ask such performance
Weigh me in your scales
Condemn me infirm beast
For such want is me
None my possession can't give
Aimless trudging and plod
Not knowing what you asked
You take time, leaving me what?
Giving that you can't return
It's a waste and waste
Look my lost flesh
Only skin my hope
What is borrowed hope?
Clinging to shadows of sunset
Tomorrow might not come
Where would joy be born
For time given to you today
Oblivion makes dark throne
Don't ask it of me
In usurpation would I grant
This were frivolous presumption

That commits to such delivery
Did you hear yet?
I don't have time

Father Less

I was once a boy and a man
Troubled a woman and father
Then tomorrow finally came
I sit out a night and wonder
Was this trouble enough today?
My own won't come home
Protesting fatherly ensemble
It was me chance upon a time
Divided of woman and children
Whose my fault was it to wonder
And sleep now won't come
A want wit and despairing man
How I would be father could I
With olive oil for wisdom talk
And opening heart only a dream
That child would treasure affection
Broken promises all good will
Littering sure path to perdition
My intended sweet intentions
Judgment is not upon intent
The act spoke to a listening house
The translation opposed heart
So supposed eagle feathers
Daggers became the night
Fathers not a choice chalice
Sometimes hemlock laced wine
Have I failed at man and father
I am sorry my fatherless children
I was father less

For a Friend

Realisation a starting point
Action follows
Forgiveness peace gives
Bitterness is a cancer
It eats from inside
Little by little must it go away
It is not a one day event
Change is inevitable
The wise embrace it
Perfect imperfections
All have had a share
Love is not love
Until you give it away
Sacrifice, Sacrifice
Correction and restoration
May you have both

Pregnant hope

I am pregnant, heavily
My steps are slow and laboured
Was is it yesterday I prayed
And light shined in my face
This time I will be delivered
Now the time is here
My water is broken
Maiweee! What pain is this
The anxiety and fear
No my water is not broken
My bladder is loose
...confused...
Birth pains grit my teeth
Perhaps it's not full term
My womb to untimely ripping
Or another still birth

Parched throat cracked lips
I will hold hope still
Mr. President the midwife
I don't know my days
Please deliver me a child

It never goes away

It never goes away
Anger, Pain, Hope
Love, Nature, Religion....
You are buffeted
It's an engulf
Till you speak
Nay maybe scream
You can't be silent
Your healing mine

Waiting game

Hide and hide again truth
My eyes shall hear in the dark
I am blind
My ears shall see the light
For, I am deaf
Fool me fool me again
I shall grow taller than your foxy ways
Your shame shall manifest
Muzzle me muzzle me again
Your yoke shall rust and break
I shall eat the fat land fruit
I see you not by sight cunning
Mistress equivocation your art
Demonic stealth your skill
Vampire bat lapping my blood
Water your garden my sweat
Stalking me in my shadow
It won't be eternity thou stink
You reek in my eyes
Revolting in my ears
The day of the pitchfork
Will entomb you just
I bear testimony true
In silence to witness
Your damnation complete
Go now, it will come around

Love dreams

I slept the other day and night too
The dreams feeding the senses
I sleep again allow my peace
Chasing a new seduction
I am not wanton like you
Yet a better flattery I follow
Hunter on my terms dictates
In secret hope colony I work
New ideas better ideals
I am seduced again no trifle
I wake up to sleep again
Dream after dream sweeter
Ideas come and go
Its performance that is wanting

Is it wanton to dream?
I have to be careful
I shan't pursue some
Seduction of thought

Dreaming

Dreaming I started young
Dreaming my hope fills
Dreaming my cares are few
Dreaming I am set free
Let mind on flight destinations real
Let mind power the surreal
Let mind conquer the formidable
Bring them home
I have been here ever
Waiting for my dreams to shadows of sunset
Tomorrow might not come
Where would joy be born?
For time given away today
Oblivion makes dark throne

Blood and Heart

This urgency coursing in my blood
Burning in me burning me
Is it the generous fullness of curvature
That surrounds your African *Godesness*
Stand still let me drink my fill of your wine
The pitchers hung full, sedate and delicate
Am a simpleton: why they are called hips!
Perhaps my blood shall curdle
Sight can't tell this feeling
Stand still don't take another step
The grace would a lynx envy your gait
Mesmerised and blinded am planted
Dare I descry the goblets prefecture
Of your full eloquent bosom
Temptress succulent and Sublime
Too delicate for my coarse peasant self
Deftly curved buds carving of Master Craftsman
Wait till they bloom in dazzling shine
What dimpled seduction I witness
Please smile again smile gently
Etched into my memory thus your lips
She laughed at my smitten stare
Smouldering double sapphire craft
Wooing Lords and Men to dream
Of Kublai Khan's damsel with a dulcimer
I have seen the song of life in your eyes
You have seen it perhaps heard it all Maya Angelou
Is it the music in the rhythm of your hips?
Or do you sing the rise and fall of your bosom?
How do you sum the treasures of your endowment

Each one silencing the other in humble submission
Yet lacking neither pronouncement nor refinement
I would, would you enslave me in your enchantments
Just to see you sing the voice of African beauty
And my hearing enthralled in a feast only for eyes
Carry mind seat a wondrous estate of my dream girl
And I, once ago, a phantom fighter renowned
Now standing, I on the bended knee of obeisance
To pay homage, to articulate invasion of my serenity
What are dreams made of for conquered hearts?
Don't stop walking your dance I join in song
Tease me to my death I carved effigy in my heart
Smile an eternal dazzle and defy my darkness
Can you see me down here on bended knee
Reaching out to kiss the hand of your glory
With uncondescending dignity of noble breeding
You offer hand, dimpled cheeks and lowered eyes
I swoon barely remembering how I got here
The fancy that you made real with no effort
Get out of my dreams get into my life.

Gift for Her

Today is a special day
And you are remembered fondly
Not least for your good looks
Not more for your sweet voice
But more because you have been
Yes, the blessing that we cherish
On the day you were born
Did they not love you with all
And with prayers wished you well
And now you stand grand statuette
Testimony to a greater Love
You have been a child since birth
Parented by God and man
And I warmed in your love too
And today is a remembrance
That you have been great and wonderful
I have neither doubt nor question
But for lack of equitable gift
Today I give you again from my heart
A gift that I cherish to whit
This prayer is my song for you
If peace be found, you in the centre of it
And all love quest, find for you a fountain
Defining success, see you mountain tops
The good of the earth, deliver you health
May your ears attune to good tidings
While your eyes see heart dreams
I know you have tasted God's sweet grace
Feel you thus His presence continually
Filling you with incense of joyous life

No, it's not your birthday perhaps
Neither maybe vogue parenting day
But that God has granted yet another
Was yesterday not just a year another day
God who stands with you today
May He stand again another year of tomorrows.
Our joys complete in yours
Not because it's Mothers' Day
But on second thoughts, why not?
Happy Mother's Day!!!

Desert

I'm used to the desert
Bare foot will be my element
Who needs your high heels?
My grace is feline
Let all cats go green
My charm is fiendish
They have called me a witch
Do I look perturbed to you?
Then please look again
Ere I send for the optician
Take a look around you
I have hiked many trails
My smooth feet gnarled inside
I have been there now here
I have climbed with them
I climb again bare foot

With no vice or avarice
I walked the deserts
Now to the mountains go
Relish it to boot its clean
Clawing at jutting rocks
Sweating a salt river
But holding firm and sure
Who said bare foot is easy
My knuckles are bare too
My heart shall not dim
The air freshly clean there
So to the top shall it be

Barefoot and knuckled
That is my element!

Thai Girl

So she said *kapunka*
That was thank you in Thai
Modesty wasn't my name
But hers was ephemeral
What had I given to merit
She is taught well
Her mother shall be proud
Words are spoken of mouth
But hers is speech of the heart
Unfeigned and uncluttered
The simplicity so cultured
One word in Thai
Preferred two in England
Who cares about language
When it's heart that speaks
Even I, untaught yokel

I know the value of one word
Kapunka means thank you
I shall treasure the sound
A word bigger than all gift
It still rings in my heart
Echoes in my motivation
A girl in Thailand said to me
Kapunka

Ego Trip

I will be a mountain yet,
You ignite my pride
Will you blame my ego?
That you did non to bruise for dampening
But fanned my fire burning coals
To lithe flaming tongues showmanship
The head is in the clouds smoky
Hairs of my insolence burn a perfidy
Do the proud enjoy being so?
Am giddy drinking the wine your praise?
Let me not tarry here long
Lest the sting of wine be my shame
Let me be a mountain to you
But please hide me under a bushel
That the world may see level ground

And you most knowledgeable
Would own what you anointed
I would only be a mountain
If that were for the humble.

She sang me

My Muse answered
I will keep, I will treasure, I will own.
The fanning is from deep down,
I will keep it glowing,
Until such a day that will be
And allow the world to test the melodies.
Though I would they taste my heart
I sang her back:
They would know your sorrow
No marvel there
It would teach peace
Self-indulgent I guess
And all in between
Fans and apologists know it all

Station

I have at a station stationed
The one was for service I stationed
They had me re-fuelled to go
And good to go passing another
The fire station attending irony
They made no fire at the place
They sat at the place usually
And prayed hope no fire
Three shifts tending non-permanent
I will drive past a third
Uniformed law enforcement
We call the police here
They have a station too
I was there once a victim
And yet once I stood offender
Some station this! no friends

Did I tell you frustration?
I made the station this other day
But missed the bus or was it train
All this on my way to another
A station of sorts daily
I work here my keep earning
They made another seat
And christened work station
I will go home and wonder
Why it too has become same
Just another station
So temporarily permanent

Have you yet been imprisoned?
In these transient stations
Then you know better
A station is not abiding
And words have no station

We all move on
Stations are temporary
Please lead me home
My daily hope...

Lies

God knows I have told my share
For fear and for gain have I dished
The gullible, the naïve, the innocent
A perfect shroud of greed and lust
Did I say God knows? As if I didn't!
Straight face, poker face read me
To think what so inspires
The baser nature of self perhaps
A true thievery of conscience
That worships self-aggrandizement
Save face today but look behind
You walk a finite chain of steel
Your crowning diamond a prison
So strong it takes the mind
Stagger in the bliss so admired
Yet the dark pervades the innards
The biggest lie needs heavy guard
The expenditure of effort resourcing
Have you seen a lie in entourage?
The whole body of it needs must cover
Till the heart at its blackest dissipates
In a cesspool of violence and pain
There is no peace even in death
For we would quake and turn
What fear is the uncovering?
Eternal victims of damnation
The lie that condemned truth
It shall be the peril of man
Sitting on the mountain of lies
Making vantage point of its peak

Neutralize any that may dig
Its foundations shake incessant
Threatening avalanche and mudslide
The cowardice of a lie makes slave
More the liar than the victim
What falls in my back quarters?
I hate the thud of a fall
My gain hangs delicate in any wind
My two eyes only one shall know sleep
My ears one shall listen to ground vibes
For, I would know who goes there
Shall peace ever be mine?
Is this the profit of a lie?

The Crushed Will Heal

Crushing under the weight of hurt
Not to squirm or worm a mite
You loaded it and sat on top
As if in parade of victory unsound
Are you ignorant or simply tyrant
It's not your toe under the press
Just another body not yours
Last night the wolves howled with me
It was full moon of my pain
And today in unrelenting heat
And villain eagle calls from pain heights
I am prey of choice
My tears are crushed out of me
My suffering voice sore reduced
In groaning heavings and sighs
In my embrace caged tightly
Yet pulverising all my essentials
Gelling a sparkling dark gem
Overwhelmed and sunk to depths
Where neither shine nor moon
Whose deliverance shall bail me
Biding my time to grow cancerous
Will eat me up before I you
This sickness not my desire
I shall strengthen my hand to mighty
Though yet still feeble I grope a start
I will set me alight of heat and pain
And in perfect glow banish the dark day
The greater the crush so shall the spark
Harness the energy my heart add it up

To melt the rock of offence breaking
That even the bruise and scar are past
The radiance of healing balm
I shall not delay my healing
This is me growing stronger
That strength that crushes
Is the strength that birthes peace anew
Perhaps someday you will claim it
With wish to roll away the tombstone
And discover the grave you buried
But now I will not tarry in dark
I will light a candle in my heart
And glow with its warmth
Then pacified wrath shall resist vengeance
Because fore given stands my reward
Singing a song of light and tranquil
Fore-giveness is spelt wrongly
Wonder why it's an hard act?
Only the givers know the healing

Dare

Open that box and take a peek inside
The blackness of charcoal of an old fire
Perhaps it was smothered in water
Perchance starved of the air
It doesn't matter now not even embers glow
Bury and forget the warmth cold season
You command not to fire the calls again
It will be understood for robbed hope
But since you opened the box
That was a march of victory begun
Now to song and drum attend
For the fire shall burn again
T'will kindle the coals hot embers
The warmth of experience to heart
Live again and ride high
Your wave has risen again

The wind is in your sails
Conquer depression season treason
There is land ahoy
That battered storm tossed ship
Land and a happy day awaiting
Only if you would dare
Light and fan the coals

To die is Human

The dryness of poverty
That scorches mouth dry
Can't afford own saliva
Hope to eat fades
This rat gnawing away
Feeding relentlessly from within
Till the dry greyness
Mere veneer covers bone
In protest jutting out
Skin can scarce hold
He is also human
And has a sister
Albeit two of them
One dying with him
And you! looking on
What's to be human?
Perhaps 'tis to die?
Then he is more human
Or to feed him
That makes you humane
The stench of death
In his wake follows
They interred his sister
There was no mourning
No one had strength
Just another of statistics
Let's play a game
Who will succumb next
The mother suckled death
The Father slept long

The flies already know
Another feast is coming
It is human to die
But humane to save?
Who has a conscience?

Treachery

One day the farmer filled his barn
An increase worth his sweat and providence
It had been a good season for returns
A fair wage paid to his hands
The barn secured against beast and man
It will be safe till trade shall be
Unbeknown a weevil and a rat
An unholy conspiracy of pests
And did a convocation at his abundance
Such unwitting magnanimity
So they bred a joyous eating brood
Such was the confident security
The farmer went to his daily bed
Waking up a day most opportune
He would his profit realise
The shock and outrage of it
Mischief performed most heinous
Why betrayal is often sneaky
And treachery is never pronounced
Rats, weevils and politicians

Protest Desperate

Nothing is silent anymore groaning all over
Sleep stands at a distance uncooperative
The throat won't allow any swallowing
The teeth in death grit won't part
The stomach burns in anger rumbling
Protestants have come to war
Who shall save this now soiled body
Standing there stark naked
Armed to the teeth with bare hands
Desperate chivalry of the oppressed
They can't lose this one fight
For they have nothing left to lose
The last stand of the dying dead
They cannot be killed more now

Insanity Bliss

The insane are better off
The idea that they live with no care
Innocence was once bliss land
Where did childhood go to hide?
Soft heads encased in eggshell
Fragility that begs gentle care
What have you got that is good
Stave the cares that stick hard
Running scared not dare look back
The hounds hard on the heel chase
Planning a morrow with marrow
Insanity is a refuge not sought
A gathering of treasure
May it bring your comfort yonder?
The vanity of quick wit is searched
Such a lack of wit is high wit
Sad songs often make one cry
This is the lot of man's kind
Who is better off a question stands
One who knows one who doesn't
Ignorance brings much inquiry
Who would be an ignoramus?
A legendary subject of idioms
The unhinged do not give a hoot
Life is in the wind I suppose
Blowing as it purposes
Such are the fruitcakes out there
What is to worry about tomorrow?
Today is not even over you see
To whose judgment is the summoning

That would not be more insane
The profanity of insatiate gathering
That overthrown mind possess not
A few cardboard boxes a bed?
Who cares about dress?
Aren't all naked hence gathering
Your rejoinder anger of my daring
You are crazier than your admission
I think to agree with you there
Perhaps am raving than you!
To ask the Gods to touch me
Vilify and perish the thought
Would one just learn the lesson
That the untaught seem to know
Today would be the day to be happy
Each in lack of accomplishment
Embrace a new madness
A real need elusive happiness

Was happy poor

Are we not worse for being better?
It was a walk in a compound
Shanty place forgotten of civilization
A toddler stark naked come to play
What is the shame of the happy?
Blissful content the brother's embrace
The magical innocence and solemnity
Remnants of cloth struggles to cover
But the fight is lost to bare buttocks
My madness thinks to cover the flesh
But the young hearts clothe in joy
Stop me in my tracks a fool
How are the poor so better dressed!
They touched with less care
Who is really happy in this world
Able to live moment by moment
Tomorrow is the only future
But for a truth, life is in effect now

History hysteria

For the life of me let me rant
Am I not also insensible
Yet in despite, am sensitive
There is no shortage of reason
Even for the fool in me
It was only yesterday's gathering
It was not the first you guessed
A sombre ceremony in depression
Took back seat - mind seat
Witnessing the introductions
Some most destitute of heart
Veiled yet most blatant self-glory
Testified their late beneficence
I would scratch my dismay
It is always an historic event this
Not so much the empty pomp
Yet history is told and rewritten
In new light we see the past
Had we then been so blind then?
Ay are we all blindly ignorant
And comes thus an introduction
That we may know them that are gone
An exaltation of bones and carrion
Testimonials to actors departed
So history is introduced of small actors
Now their magnificence larger than life
Perhaps it was for granted
An obituary to a well that's now dry
Just another memorial service
I guess we are greater in death

When we have been mortally humbled
Now scratch my head confusion
What was my ranting about again?
Ah yes the bland and insipid ritual
What good is an obituary
To introduce the unknown departed?
So here lies what is not anymore
The standing laud graces and gratitude
One last stand of soldiers to fall too!
An encore solidly sordid!

Agony of Love

The agony of love is not loss
For love never loses and cannot lose
How would it lose if it is giving?
For love knows not to expect
Like a clear sweet stream breaks forth
Watering grass and both beast and man
In defiance of the cloudy misty day
In rejoicing on the bright sunny day
So love pours out of self
What is loss if reserves abound
Yet it agonises, grieves and mourns
It was you the other day, now me
Tears, wipe, stream again, wipe
Would love to laugh again
How it would nourish to health
How it would quench ages of thirst
Washing it would clean without favour
Broken hearted in dejected longing
The labour of love undelivered
Heavily pregnant agony
In the night the stream flows
It's determined course following
In stormy gales feeding flow
Just one more time one more day
Just another year another jubilee
The burden of another's smile
Nay, if it could be done
Would the agony be gone!
Or would it?
Labour on?

Would sing

Grant me words most potent
I would string them together in a new song
A song you hear in your sleep at night
A song whose drum would be your heartbeat
A song that you would not hear with ears
A song that you would feel in your bones
That song would never grow old
And the tune would only be known to you
A song that only my heart could sing
Would make that song your anthem of ages
To serenade you under the stars of heaven
Would the melody carry you to distant parts
In lands where not even one has dreamt
And there create a sanctuary for you
A serene and most blissfully abundant land
Nay that land does exist most deep
Watered and tended in my heart
Come, the band is starting
It is your song, our song
The lyric is me

Book for Africa

I want to write a book
A book for Africans about Africa
That talks of the violent sands of Sahara
And the raging serpentine Nile in the North
The uncompromising Zambezi in the South
I want to talk about the golden sunrise
The fiery noon of equator and its dark violence in the sky
That sunset which heralds dark things
Nocturnal insects and deadly predators
The moonlit skies of autumn Savana
The forgotten serenity of debt free existence
That sat upon fortunes and treasure
Hid in the vast expanses of Africa
The gentle scents of our fauna
Which called out hornets instead of bees
Plundered African nectar and dealt treachery
As paedophiles lure with candy and toy
They said sodomy was a crime
Gleefully they went to commit
What will be the title of my African story
And the shame to use this borrowed tongue
Which scarce describes the drum and dance
Vehement resistance of the assegai
The impassioned battle cry "bulala abatakati"
Now diseased and bereft of identity
Africa on course of synthetic cultural antibiotic
That kills anything African for modernity
Creating a history so black not for nature
But charred remains of once sacrosanct beauty
I can't write now, For we stand at the graveside

Here bent to inter bony remains
That superior maggots gnawed and cleaned
The stench of rot and lost pride of *ubantu*
Yet a remnant was left what little hope
An awakening an arising a rebirth
Revival of a people of peoples
To a black Renaissance thwarted to date
They will read the story on their way
Of a subjugation of a race once great
History is written by victors they say
So are lies shoved down our throats
Savage brush paints our sacred culture
Which taught complimentary responsibility
Now equity avowed baptising competition
There are winners; and winners and losers
Demoncracies elevated to religious platform
Upholding the folly of majority
An abdication of accountability
So the blind lead is led blind by multitudes
Common good makes truth minority
Let's agree friends fun is fiend unsatiated
So Africa inundated with Disney contraptions
Keep Timon and Pumba having jungle fun
Then appropriate value with kids at play
They will come home for a cookie dog
Tired and dreaming of adventure
Sleep overtakes the eyelids
The blind do see better sometimes
I said I want to write a letter to Africa
Which shall shake her slumber out
Give her feet so her bones walk again
Pulling her earth for new sinews

Cover the bones to strength anew
See how your milk waters wide earth
Yet only the dregs of rot feed yours
Your generous udder a cash cow
Whose profit flies day and night
Leaving carvenous ruin and traps
Swallowing in the depths of greed and lust
Those that would dare stand at battlements
Mayibuye iAfrica a sound that's now taboo
What would we be without beneficiation
Cold calculating ruthless cunning
Take their identity away keep the soul
A souvenir in a calabash you drink from
Are you a people yet for pride and power
The real bastion and defence eroded
Hear me Africa though I am no Prophet
Open your eyes - your ears - profit
Is it for want of sons that you wallow
Murky waters of poverty wash your brow
Having married off your sons like daughters
The trinkets you received for dowry
Even your name has changed
But remember where you don't belong
The new order of this earth
You the hewer of wood and beast burdened
The letter will say go to the hills
Listen to the stones awakening in the wind
Hills fill the valleys and let unity drum sound
Our mountains will roar and be heard
A behemoth shall come from the setting sun
And push the darkness back northward
Stock the labour pains a rebirth

A union of the order of Gondwana
That made nations quiver and quake
The tectonics of power start here
A single mind, a heart, a hand
Sleep not my children lest you are stolen
And sold into eternal bondage
Dream on your feet you Africa
My letter is not written till you write it
African child the author of destiny
Please write a new book our story
The book I write by your hand
Going back to the future in Africa
There you will read the story

Don't fade hero

When the magma chamber boiled
A cauldron of anger and pain broil
A foment of repression oppressed
What steam pot would hold together
My word! Would things so fall apart
Mountains bursting asunder
And vehement debris toss high
In plumes of fire smoke and sulphur
Mountain shaken Vulcan spoke
The ashes spread far and wide
Mountains covered pyroclastic flow
A burning revolution snaking downhill
The anger of my kin a reckoning come
The charred remains would testify
Memorials cut in granite and alabaster
The revolution birthed the evolution
The angry ash of agony enriching the soil
So a son of the soil till land to crop
Was the great hope nursed in magnanimity?
Burying races and to race no more
Was the stuff of his, your dream?
Retractors detractors lay in ambush
In subtlety to contrive demise of this hope
Tis perfidy such refraction of purpose
Refractors galore reflectors most lacking
The African dream, Western anathema
A nemesis to such treasonous intent
The singular sin never to be a colony again
The neighbour loves a woman my wife
He will chop my head off, for to bed her!

What are you all looking at now?
The writhing almost lifeless body of dreams
We lie in death throes in bloody treachery
And Brutus my brother betrays you for a morsel
You will to Egypt again and die in wine dining
Bob was not Moses and Tango not Aaron
Joyful was not the music of Miriam turned mourning
Difference turned deference in reconciled mission
The promise is a heritage of the resilient
Did Caleb and Joshua not war divide the spoil?
Now the quake has hit seven on Richter's measure
A shock of silence that rocks the world
Every babe's mouth has a tale some so banal
Eulogies and epitaphs un-ululated recitals
Some for show and profit many coy and false
Friends, Africans, Anglicans and countrymen
I have come to entomb Bob and not praise him
Lest I incur the ire and wrath of Charming sons
This Rob did he not deliver us a dream
Yet a son calls him villain, and this Son a good man
I am not Mark of the Anthony brood
Neither is Bob chipped of the rock of Caesars
But listen you the four winds speak unison
Which of us here having drunk power are sober
Are we not inebriates in one multiple misdemeanour
While horrid heart play judge and jury equivocation
Vile have turned the fruits of our adversity
Having bathed the baby, we throw it with bath water
Once a darling and espouses were eloquent
Our dark man with white entrails Lord Soames says
Dealing us another Lobengula trick
Thus the history of colonial trickery repeated

So slept they with inner man till Blair toiletry was found
And turned the sweetheart inside out
White painted sepulchre of your ancestral trickery
Amazing impropriety of your prostitution
Who props up killers and despots for his profit?
Question presider Johnson on Vietnam South
Sanctified Santos thievery thwarting resented Marxists

Throw your enemy to the anaconda's hunger
And your onetime friend under the bus
Let go speech find another day
When burial dust is finally and finely settled
A book of your exploits be written emblazoned
An indelible mark that shall not fade
For the life of a nation even in abject denial
Your shadow will be taller than your days
This is not a course of apologetics
Mugabe, for lacking praise
Don't fade
Hero
Yes

...After thought

The hills of power reverberating in discord
Far and near the echo will be for terms and ages
Only yester year he stood at arms gallant
Inspiration that spoke juggernaut determination
To educate freed minds and grow nationhood
Today bears testimony diaspora beneficiaries
The vatic sinner lies caked sans breath
No, I do not judge fair but are you standing just?
Am I the one seeing yet am sand blind?
Dark conspiracy hemmed you in blindfold
After having cause that you, him, then some still
Is it not a fairness; (not of skin) to moan this departure
In halls of learning such serious expose
It was just the fury of a midget
Forgive such as dream thus

Kindler

Bring the billows to the fire place
The coals are yet black and volatile
Ignition will come fire starter
Pyrokinesis is your middle name
There was a writer loved his muse
Was she not the daughter of Tobela
And he only the lesser sibling
Come then stoke the fire
Till the labour of the coal is red-hot
The blast from these bellows a fiery fury
The coals birth screaming flames
Let ambition's labour break waters
Give birth to this dream
It was in the pressure and heat
A force bequeathing diamonds
Come then press me harder
Burn me and kindle a river
A spring that shall be drunk
Only by the hardened palate
Vessels forged in earthenware
Whose resilience is tested in fires
Carry the reason of ages forgotten
Fetch some met for babies lips
The spring scalds iron and bronze
The non-geothermic insolence of thought
Make way for inevitable catharsis
Then history shall note this non event
And the giants will laugh aloud

Mountain afar off

We reckoned them blue the mountains afar
The hills in the distance were green
They conjured breath taking visions
Such delicate and sublime defiance
Commitment strapped hikers boots
To be swallowed a speck in the expanse
Would risk all for momentary intimacy
The great seduction intoxicating
To be delivered only in the reach
Finally making the foot hills
The aura captured in green cologne
The musk of green, rot and explosive bud
The ascent is slow and deliberate
Reality check broken boulders
A dear trail barely visible guesses a path
Mushroom growth on trunks rotting
Then there the bones cleaned forgotten
A scattering of dung who knows by what
Where is the magnetic beauty?
Close range tell a story real
Often more pungent than distance speaks
Oratory of the politicians
The hill and mountains are indeed beautiful
But that is a trick of distance
Nice from afar off
Truth far from nice
Yet even in the rot they carry
The green finds its life
Fertilizing the soil making the hills smile
The colour in the distance hypnotic

Drawing our kind always to this lust
To touch the beautiful things
Mountains and hills beautiful in the distance.

Want out went in

Where do people go when they want out
Was it ill advisement to desire in
Is there yet another place that's not in
These questions are they not packed
Is this not the melancholy of foolishness
How do I get out to get in again
To run out of this in, takes me a place
Into the irony of another in
The bronze enamelled feet of resolve
Trades me a slave to be harnessed in bonds
Is man not the proverbial prisoner
Breaking walls fast building new faster
Is it not the same mortar and stone
How many outings are not innings

This sport most horrid unbeatable foe
Creates the game rules plays umpire
The goal post always shifts against me
Tails the beast wins and heads I lose again

Deceived

The joke is on me another time
My opponent is a shape shifter
With uncanny devilry resides my core
Now my hearty my arch-deceiver
Said that it was inwards upon a time
Now I ask back ultimate fool me
What is outside of this inside
Was it another drunken consummation
The joke is on me in all over again

Weakness of the strong

The humble are weak
For strength is not understood
The loud are strong
That's because they are heard
What is strength than beating self down
What is weakness but raging vocals
The strong bring to life
But the weak fill the graves
Weakness of humility is strength of control
Fumes of incontinence drive anger
Teach the ear to see strength
And the eye will listen better
I am beat up by me not you
It is not cowardice to allow them life
Soon they will know it
Eating humble pie

Today a prayer and song

Today when writers are quiet
And the poets sit silent
In reverend gratitude to God
But their hearts quiver in song
As they join in silent noise
Connected in joyful unison
To echo your joy in the distance
We celebrate with you
The days that turn years
And our faith pray another three
Each term 30 making four
A fullness of years that's our wish
Flagons of joy be always full
And you drink as you flourish
From success to victory
May your ride be sure footed
In boots cobbled in wisdom
Grace watering your pathways
With gentleness of morning dew
Keeping you humble in your rise rise
Would I wish for anything
That was in my power to give
Then this day it would be yours
Yet I know one who has abundance
To Him I have lifted my words
He hearing shall say "I Will".
This far has He stood by you
Walking in front to guide your steps
God of love loving you endlessly
Keeping you in the hollow of His hand

Keep faith oh child for He is not done
It's a truth; He has just started with you
And the plan will unfold
Keep your station and see His hand
Mighty in battle is the Lord
He knows the thoughts he has toward you
Never harming you in the least
Yes prospering you and giving hope
Now as I sing this song to you
My heart speaks another word
That your ears can't hear
For its a prayer to Him
To grant the desire of your heart
The poets and writers are silenced
But hear my song for you
"I, LOVE YOU TOO"

Thieving watchers

Watchers and hypocrites abound
I have two neighbours
One watching my front porch
Knows all arrivals and departures
One has eyes on my backyard
You would think he's got my back
My departures are all timed
They break the party on my return - just
They will continue when my back is turned
A stranger house breaker, all man hate
A smiling thieving friend is the worst
Then you have him for a neighbour
Through the back door makes daily entry
Plundering my stash refreshing on my sweat
And my conniving front neighbour keeps peace
Complicit in knowledge and abatement
The back watcher is my brother by election
He sleeps with the woman across my street
And she invites me to dinner and caviar
The art of being neighbourly mastered
High sounding principles uttered all evening
Liberty, equality, justice and brotherhood
The moral high ground the worst is West
At my revelling drunkenness my backdoor is opened
Who watches the watcher that is bought
Ingratiating the hand: that pilfering hand
The watcher has an army of robbers
Feigning humanist rhetoric from a vantage point
Slowly to my knees I succumb
My brother, agent of my subjugation

The story North's love of the South

The Watering

I have seen your tears
Tears that spoke loneliness
I have seen your tears
From a broken fountain of love
I have seen your tears
The vicissitudes of life
I have seen your tears
Yet you stand not broken
I have seen your tears
Tears that mould you strong
I have seen your tears
You are not killed, your are stronger
I have seen your tears
You cried yesterday night
I have seen your tears
You cried this morning
I have seen your tears
And I have seen the strong you
You will cry tomorrow
That I am sure of
You will cry tomorrow
When you come to harvest
You will cry tomorrow
With full basket and abundance
Your tears that watered the ground
And refreshed the barren land
Has turned a desert to oasis
Your tears that fed little birds
A heart that would only give
Will cry tears of joy for sure reward

Nakedness

The naked we, are naked
There is nakedness of one
Then another manner of nakedness
All speak to the lack of covering
Loins testify the physical want
A past that has been unkind
That future event may can fulfil
This is not of sad report
There is hope for this humanity
There is nakedness so wanton
Bereft of virtue, in substance of vice
Revelry gilted in glitter and pomp
The singular pursuit of one too many
Noticed with the rising of day
Undimmed by setting night
Ambition and lust rule supreme
A sad day is upon the sun
A nakedness so callous
Hiding cannibal canines in smiles
The good news of democracy
Alas many choose what few keep
So happily to their unholy phylacteries attend
This nakedness deliberate is another
On beaches uncovered fun
A nakedness deliberate sunbathe
An offence of flesh bordering perversity
Nay, its your body
It is this other nakedness
The one deep inside the being
Coursing in the veins a cursing

Corruption so hardening heart
And they have no shame
Undressed to kill

The Heart is Inside

That would not be good where it not
We still carry our hearts inside,
And inside the hearts dreams
We honour God today, sometimes,
Yet we are loaded inside,
True hearts will speak our hope
And true hearts speak our pain
What shall we say then?
Don't forget to love
Never love to forget
A heart forgetting to love dies
A heart loving to forget dries
A heart that loves remembers
It loves and laughs

That one I carry inside
That one carries you!
A seat your forever throne
You rule, you rule
Not to be forgotten

Scribbled in a Tank

Last night I slept in a tank
They had put me in there
Cramped foetal position and all
Hell there is comfort yet?
I was tanked for the speaking
That the system had tanked
Like the tanked village they run
So they had me tanked too.
No pillow for to comfort
And they shoved bricks at me
A head rest so hideous to sight
Marked in vitriolic sounds of fear
It stinks in the tank sir
I choke in the anguish of scribes
Who labour to undo my bonds
Scarce their scant efforts prevail
Once was thanked but now tanked
They muzzle a calf milking mother cow
So harsh visitation was upon the day
That saw me being tanked
Bones, flesh and blood they had me
Muffled my screams to slow death
The earth watching in amazement
As the pen killers swallowed pain killers
So I pulled my hand for a pillow
And my foetal saliva and tears dried
Into indelible ink on pillow of pain
The only comfort for my broken body
To know that the mind is unbreakable
Silence of the lambs for the abattoir

Slowly I liquefied and found balance
Moulded to the tank as waters
The waters won't rust but your tank will
The words of my liquid brain will seep
And cause many plants to grow
Green and resilient multitudes
You will need many tanks Your Excellency
Till you run out iron to make more
And they will come for you
To broom clean and shovel your casket
The word came from the tank
You put me in there speechless
The writing on my pillow-hand behold
Has become written on your wall
And your great want for pain killer
As made you that pen killer
You tanked your soul
Your freedom is free-doom
I will pass by Hell just to see you.

Scared of Goofy

My dog died a few years ago
The sign is at my gate still
Beware of the dog: he is vicious
A reputation he had upheld
Diligent barking on world fora
My neighbour still has his Goofy,
A Saint Bernard all toothy
Giant he is striking fear in many
Who dares count his teeth?
Yet a few are in the know
A boy caught in his jaws only yesterday
Wet from Goofy's drool
Cried of horror at the monster
Picked up half dead by his dad
A little bath and hug from mum heals all
A few people know too
They read the epitaph
Memories of a fallen canine
The sign still at my gate
Has become the butt of many jokes
Say mate, how about a new sign
Beware of my dead dog: was he vicious!
Howdy neighbor: how about it
You take the epitaph to pet cemetery
Might keep intruders off hallowed ground
And my son, witty and all, says
He might be dead, but his kin aren't
So, BEWARE! A joke?
Yet for all these of clever sassiness
Others pass my neighbour's revered abode

Tread they softly mighty Goofy is nearby
Ignorance has power over men
To cause trembling before statuettes
It dawned to me then true revelation
A present dog - toothless one
Stands mightier than a dead savage
So I said I will get a new dog
Canines, claws, bark and all
And new sign for my gate
"Have Upgraded to New Dog.02"
"Teeth, claws and bark factory installed!"
Next plebiscite is in five years
The difference between toothy and no dog?
Listen to the boy's voice of experience!
Lots of bark, no bite!
Version New Dog
Upgrade or repackage

How did We get Here?

I sat there and wondered
How did we get here
Just another poor man thinking
Yet more urgent was my status
Would I test positive
Positive thoughts now
Positive is positive that's good right?
And sat nonchalantly - I think
Hoping for negative
Negative is the new positive
So now there are two sides
Once positive was good
Now, negative is better!
The world is in a mess
Hardly affording the fee
But had to test anyways
Just 55USD: did I say just?
So I did a head count to a dozen
Not bad business for the hour
That's definitely positive
Got me thinking sadly
Brother in-law battling for life
That would take tests
Medicines would be prescribed
Ah business is good for some
Would they hate COVID19?
Was this not their boon
How did we get here sir?
Is there a dame to answer me?
The prophet did not see it come

The shaman is in a daze
The scientist is reeling confused
This one smiles at the bank
Raving rude reality
Was it the bat that ate pangolin
Was it man who ate bat
Or some mad Einstein's lab work?
How did we catch this one
WHO can find answers?
Is there really a Chinese connection?
How did we get here?
Who am I asking – sigh, sigh again?
My turn came a little paperwork
Stick an cotton bud up my breather
Eyes closed I squirm a bit
Wriggle, wriggle, wriggle and three more
Is this how we die now?
Go wait outside and pay up
She could have been friendlier
Stuff their pockets
Perhaps they deserve it
I will go my ways forgotten
Perhaps that's positive
But I will remember for long
And ask again
How did we get here?

God please SMILE

Coming naked and clenching little empty hands
A baby loved most when least is deserved
A cry that would be followed by many more
And that was the announcement of arrivals
You had become my mother and I your baby
If I could I would remember your first look
Your first cuddle over my delicate being
Would I still on my little shoulders feel today
And lips of love kissing my untaught indifference
Assurance rang a whisper 'twill be ok!
Now that I was out of watery grave liberated
The journey would be long and arduous
The race would not be the fast
It would be a test of endurance
And I totally oblivious of the magnitude of your toil
Carried in dark to full term
The light was darkness till my learning started
And a world of forms began all around
An explosion of puzzles as a maze of crazy
Mind crawled as would my body and you were there
And faithful teacher you were ordained
To hold little hands aiding my ungainly legs
To take my first step was your doing
And now many more have followed running
I am still the bundle you delivered and you still here
Could I repay your sacrifice I would
But where would I start to count the cost
And what date would mark the end
Whose currency would give true value
And what scale would you put weighing mothers love

Just for the nine months you would be worthy
But for you that was not all you gave
Just for My first song and my first word
Would I give you the world and be still in debt
You stopped not with my walking song but dolled more
Look at me Mother do you see well
I have become taller than you - what childish glee
Was it part of the plan you would be shorter
You have watched me grow from shrub to tree
Sit woman in the shade you natured and nurtured
Do you see them counting me mama
I have waxed strong and have increased
I am that which you have made with love
As a potter moulded his mind's desire
But have I not shamed your grace with my truancy?
The tears you have cried when I was wayward
Washed me dry and decanting the bath water
The water and stink of my shame and forgotten
The fragrance of her love in perennial bud
My shade is too small for the giant that my mother is
Like your babe that I have always been
Winter come in your sunshine I bask
And hot summer are u not my shade
In humbled adoration my prayer today
God grant these mothers a long life
For who deserved more?
God gracious and loving please
SMILE
SUSTAIN
MOTHERS
IN (your)
LOVE

(so) ENDLESS.

Do Now, Tomorrow Comes

My years have passed by quietly
I have taken me places with many
Traversed lands and seen things
The vast karoos, the imposing Kilimanjaro
Sailed waters: walled Kariba and free seas
Made peace with waters serene
And tossed in devil tides of the deep
The air had the freedom of the wind
High fliers go above the clouds
Sublime carpet under their wings
So here is to those who are travelled
That have seen beauty in lands and people
And braved rough *see* challenge
To testament of the Eagle song
Do yours and do you .... please
Travel: sail, fly make a fortune
Spend money, be happy
There is a journey that lasts
One that is shorter than all
And they take you remnant
(And your raiment also)
Making a safe deposit
Stand me by the door
Behold the solitude
Dad taken there
Some place
A journey
Final.

Am I Happy

Am I happy?
Perhaps not!
I am angry
Very angry
Am in anguish
Deep anguish
I am hungry
Sore hungry
I am cold
Freezing cold
You find me in the street
Painting graffiti on walls
I am here snatching purses
Sleeping under that bridge
Cajoling for price cut
For a rotting darkened banana

You think I chose this?
Are you not the peddlers
And pushers my misfortune!
A stinking dirty pauper, me
You are quick to forget
We came here together
You said you knew the way
My shoulder bore your weight
You had the eyes for my blindness
I didn't know then
That donkeys and horses
Are housed at the stables

The cosy mansions
Belong to the riders
Donkeys and horses good
But the riders more excellent
Here waiting your benevolence
To chance a bundle of hay
My prayer for daily bread
If Boxer and Benjamin had brains
Would they discern Piggy's bunch
Fattened in our dire crunch
But would they stop the drag?
Strike a blow on Napoleon
Not the French man *hero*
Not George Orwell's making either
But the one setup we in ballot
Look closer home
Benjamin opened his eyes
Too late for Boxer
But as for this Napoleon
But as for this Napoleon
As for this Napoleon
Run him out of Animal Farm!
Run him out of town!
We... We belong here!

Grave Thoughts

Grave thoughts often visit me
Snaking their way uninvited perversion
So eloquent and obtuse to finite thought
What if I could speak from the grave!
Would I know the living tongue?
Would the children of life listen?
Why are poets not singing posthumous?
But perhaps I will write from beyond
As I repeat the story immemorial
That painted sepulchres do not sing
Their glory outrage of rotting carrion
The poem of feasting polity worms
This is not so grave after all
Why do we in such finesse and art
Crack and grave flint rock
Just to mark soiled and mottled
Remnants a similitude we all take
The victor is not the grave either
The worm feast will feed a new worm
Till only scarred granite remains atop
A memory chiselled in stone
It too will be forgotten
Till in chancy encounter bones speak
An interpretation of archaeological thought
Finally I will write from the grave
A story I can not answer for
Don't mock me fellow
This is grave melancholy

Solomonic Lust

Solomon's lust who could match
Epic proportions unsurpassed of man
You deign it good he tasted and tested
What curious thought drove him hard
Far and wide spread aroma wisdom
Far and wide his tentacles touched
Hearts did he break hundreds count
Is the good man bad? let me rephrase
Was the bad man good to touch so much?
And then came the knowledge of vanity
O for the cynical - vanity of vanities
The world haves have their desires
Yet none of us is satisfied
Philanthropy; is it not over rated
For still the lust for more is unquenched
Donald still blows a Trump-et seeking
Power makes wealth or wealth power
A spiralling cycle says this little wisdom
Bill-ion Gates all golden would seek more
So man touches taboo and it's normal
The vanity of man was Nimrod's babel
Babbling has not stopped the lustful
So Egypt ramped up pyramids
Were the Aztecs and Inca not mighty?
Is Great Zimbabwe not chiselled stone?
A ruin and ruins shall man pursue
The lust to conquer highest heights
Who are our neighbours in space
The horn hungers for conquest
This lustful flesh is man's kind

And Solomon was he not a ruin
Yet, aspiration of many, if to surpass!

King's Humbling

Mighty empowered Your *High Knees*
Nay Your Lordship the *tongue sleeps*
I mean slips not Knees Your *HighNess*
You are King over us motley fools
Laughing at my conjecture of your honour
Do imaginings warrant confession and sentence?
A King is such to a Kingdom
A King is only a king to a people
Nations will quake and tremble
When Kings sit on their throne
Their sceptre determine life or death
Such is the power of them who rule
In state streets and palace doors
Regal rulers flash and flaunt their power
How the deprived would touch his hand
Ask for mercy and perhaps a morsel
They have power to take and give
And yet in chambers deep
In the wake of the dark nights
Witness the humbling of the King
The regal crown and royal robes
Hanging in a pile on the floor forgot
Indeed, to a woman, the King is man
Dressing him nakedness
To whimper, groan, scream and swear
And so, the woman rules the man
And you out there, you honour the King
In day Kings and Power will parade
Vent words ominous endearing and threatening
Such are these double faced Januses

Think tonight coming undress and nudity
See their happy puppy dance of humiliation
None would I imagine greater caricature
When the power meets a woman
Of course no ringside seats tonight!

Not so quiet

This is me
My silence is dark
My silence is deep
Sevens of fathoms deep
64 Black shades dark
Not 32 bit mind
It screams pain
Does it not roar rage
Keep thinking

The mayhem in board games is seen by the pieces. The players shake hands and contest another day. Such is politics.

Forward

The Grass is Fighting

Of *coup detats* and stolen elections
I have seen a few hypocrites prosper
Ambivalent vocalists of democracy
To wild cheers and adulation
They stage a dream and sell a lie
They will be high on power drug
Coke and heroin may pale in power
Alas the addicts only crave more
Will they not pilfer, rob and kill
Chiefs of staff become Thieves of stuff
Who hears my voice in the din
I can't even hear me in the furore
My neighbours each side gathered
Cheering their chief performer
My whiskers, it's rubbing on to me
I should have said of chief; thief and forcer
Let our band get the accolades
So rages confrontation of dreams
Only it's not our band at all
We the entranced fanatical audience
True I was a follower too yesterday
Till sobriety overtook opioid use
So my neighbours are still at it
Yesterday the streets were littered
Broken bottles of failed molotovs
Spent missile rocks another failed riot
My neighbours are at it again today
Whose throat will be slit first?
Their voice vanquished to silence
It does not matter much though

For our alphas become our terror
Their sunrise sees our last song
As another dark night begins
And return again vicious victims
Let the wind carry my sigh
My neighbours have stopped their ears
The deaf attending the party of the blind!
Alas, the grass and trees are fighting
The veld is set on fire
Elephants
Glorified
Still graze the charred remains

Have you ever stood in the wind alone
Howling winds hit your face
Till your tears are blue
The critic has greater licence
The poet shredded in silence
Smarter than your emotion
Wiser than your reason...

Don't miss out!

Visit the website below and you can sign up to receive emails whenever Forward H Makwavarara publishes a new book. There's no charge and no obligation.

https://books2read.com/r/B-A-LXCCB-RSCSC

BOOKS 2 READ

Connecting independent readers to independent writers.

Also by Forward H Makwavarara

Howling Winds and Blue Tears

About the Author

Born a village boy in 1969, the last of five siblings, Forward Makwavarara fell in love with literature at a tender age of 6years, in first grade, thanks to the reading siblings he has. The first poem that made a permanent impression on Forward was "Bongwi" by Kingsley Fairbridge. In secondary school Forward started writing his own poetry for fun. In "Howling Winds and Blue Tears", the poet explores a wide range of themes with the passionate often melancholic voice of protest poetry. The protestant pleads for nature, the poor and oppressed and the child among other things. The honesty and the passion in this anthology makes one to reflect on both the ills and the good in society. Much as there is rebuke of society, poet does not spare himself but he also calls himself out!